CLASSIC FAIRY TALES

Illustrated by Rachel Swirles

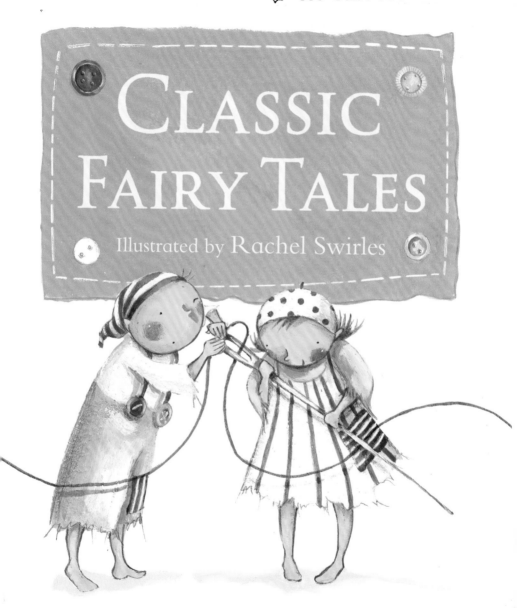

Retold by Lucy M George

meadowside
CHILDREN'S BOOKS

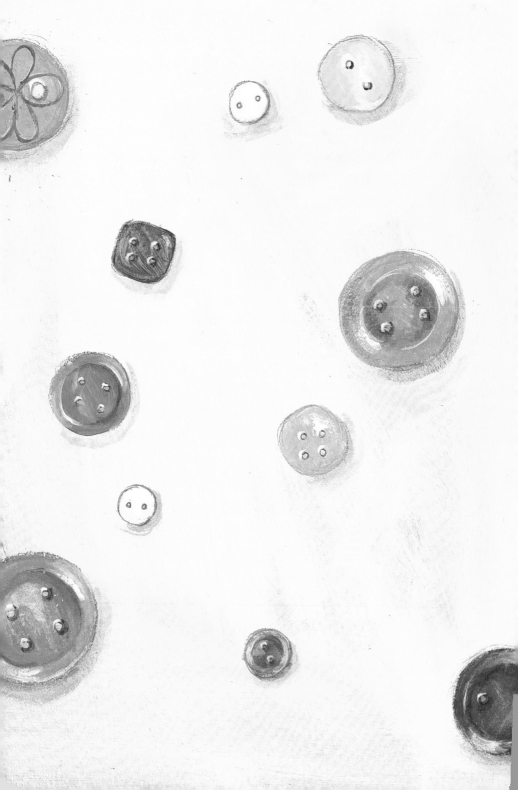

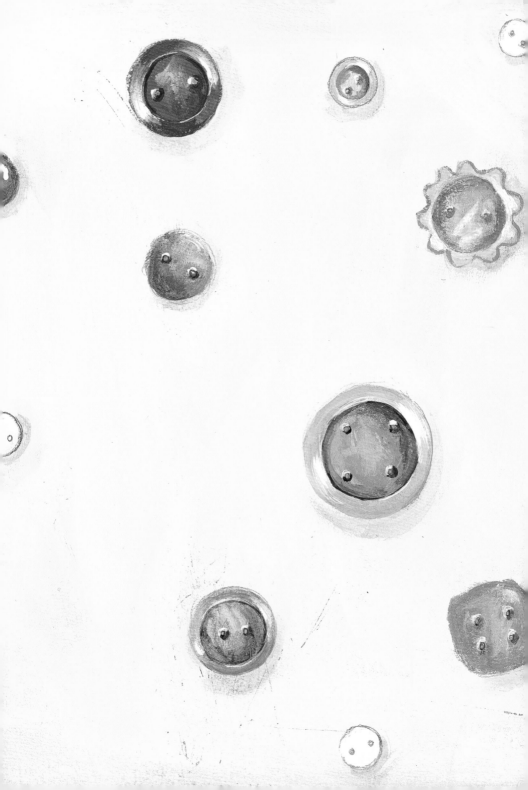

thumbelina

Retold by **Lucy M George** and illustrated by **Rachel Swirles**

There was once a tiny little girl who was
no bigger than a thumb. She was called
Thumbelina. She lived in a beautiful
flower in a warm and happy house.

On bright mornings she would row across
the milk bowl, with a whistle and a giggle as
she went, smiling and happy with the world.

But one day, as she slept beside
the window…

...a nasty toad mother crept up and snatched her!

She trapped Thumbelina on a lily leaf, too small to swim home, too afraid to call for help.

The toad mother was going to make
Thumbelina marry her horrid toad son!

As Thumbelina's tears splashed into the pool,
the fish looked up and saw how lovely
she was. They had to help.

So they nibbled and they gnawed through
the stem of the lily, until the leaf floated free.

"Oh thank you, thank you!"
she called as she floated away.

But as she drifted, she realised that she
was going further and further away from
her home.

Suddenly, a mayfly landed on her leaf.
Without even saying 'hello', it poked her
and said, "My, my! You are a pretty little
thing, I think I shall take you back to
my family."

"Oooh! It has no wings," said the mother.
"Ergh! It has no feelers," said the brother.
"Yuk! It only has two feet," said the sister,
"and it is so ugly!"

They cast Thumbelina from their tree.

Winter had come and Thumbelina was all
alone in the world. Great snow flakes fell
and the ground grew colder.

Shivering and hungry, Thumbelina lay
on the frozen ground and wept. Just as
she was falling into a deep, deep sleep…

…she felt a warm breath upon her face.

When she awoke, she found herself in the
home of a field mouse.

He had saved her life and Thumbelina
would be eternally grateful.

She and Mouse spent the whole winter together, happy in his cosy little home.

Beside the merry little fire they were safe and warm from the frosty winds outside.

That winter, every afternoon, Thumbelina
would walk with Mouse to visit his friend
Mole for a cup of tea and homemade cakes.

They had a splendid time and Mole began
to grow rather fond of Thumbelina.

Mouse was so kind to Thumbelina, but she soon found that he wanted her to repay him.

The following year, Thumbelina would have to go and live with Mole in his dark underground hole!

One day on the way to Mole's, Thumbelina
heard a crying from the frosty earth above.

She crept to the surface and there, she found
a small bird, lying in a tangled nest of twigs
and leaves.

"I was too tired to fly with my friends
this winter," cried the poor swallow.

So Thumbelina visited Swallow secretly everyday, taking him seeds and water to make him strong again.

Very soon, they became the best of friends. And over the seasons that followed he

slowly got better and better. Until eventually,
Swallow was strong enough to fly away.

"I will never forget you!" he cried.
"And I will never forget you!" she said.

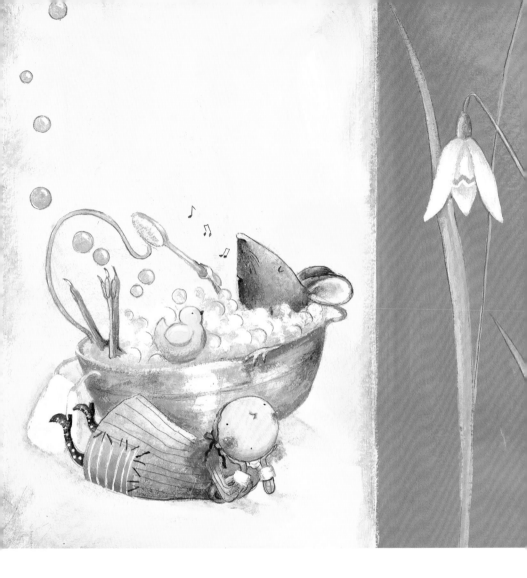

And she didn't.

But she missed him. And since he had gone, Thumbelina had spent all of her days inside with Mouse. And now, the time had come to go and live with Mole in his dark underground hole.

Thumbelina longed to see the sky one more time, so she crept out early one morning whilst the ground was still soft. A tear rolled down her cheek.

"Goodbye, flowers!" she said sadly.

Suddenly, a bird landed beside her.

"Why are you crying?" he asked.
"Because," she wept, not looking up,
"I have to marry an old, blind mole tomorrow
and I'll have to live underground forever…"

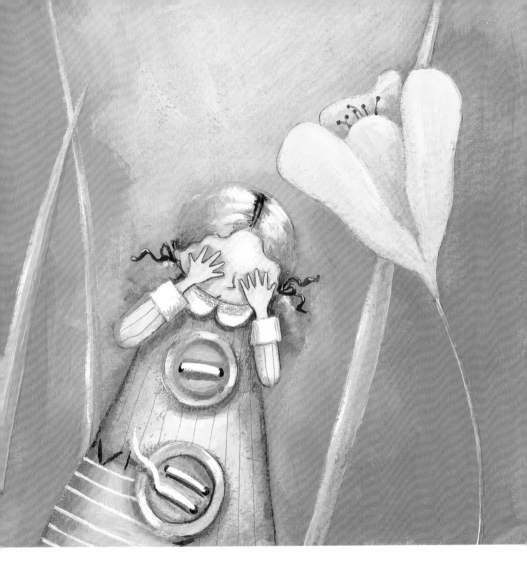

He smiled and then, laughing gently,
he said, "Thumbelina, it's me!
Your old friend, Swallow! You once saved
me and now I can save you!"

Thumbelina threw her arms around his
neck and held on tightly. Then they took
off and soared away from all her troubles.
Over mountains, past babbling brooks
and through fields, dotted all over with
wild and colourful flowers.

She felt alive again! Everything looked so
small from the air that Thumbelina forgot how
small she was and started to feel strong again.

Then Swallow called out to her,
"Pick a flower! That is where you shall live."

As they swooped towards the ground,
Thumbelina saw a beautiful white flower.

"That one!" she pointed.

But as she fell softly into the flower,
Thumbelina gave a little cry of surprise.
For right there, in the middle was...

The Prince of the Fairies!

Swallow waved goodbye with a promise
to visit her every spring.

See you
next
spring!
Love
Swallow x

And so, at last, Thumbelina had
found her home.

The
Snow Queen

Retold by Lucy M George and illustrated by Rachel Swirles

In a little town, not so far from here,
lived a boy and a girl. They were best friends
and their names were Kay and Gerda.

Kay and Gerda lived next door to one
another. From their windows they
would play games and pass secret notes.

They would talk all day, (and sometimes
whisper all night). Everywhere they went,
they went together. Everything they did,
they did together. And every secret they had,
they told each other. Every single one.

Kay loved the spring and Gerda loved
the autumn, but both of them loved
the winter.

At the first sight of snow, they would drag
Kay's wonky old sledge to the hill and then
ride it all the way to the frozen lake,

falling off into the soft snow and laughing
as they went.

When it was cold enough the lake froze so
thick that the children could skate upon it.

One day, some of the older children started talking about an evil queen. A queen who lived in the frozen hills. A queen who lived in a palace of ice. The Snow Queen.

"She comes down here to steal children," said the oldest boy.

"She blows enchanted snow into your face,
then you have to go with her."

"My grandmother told me she steals you from
your bed and you can never come back because
she makes you so cold, you forget who you
are and where you live," said another one.

Kay was scared of the stories about the Snow
Queen and he told Gerda on the way home.

"Nothing could ever make me forget you!"
promised Gerda. "Even if your heart was frozen,
and no one remembered you, and you didn't
even know who you were! Even then...

I would remember you. I promise!"

And so they carried on up the hill,
throwing snow, laughing and dreaming of
the hot chocolate that awaited them at home,
all thoughts of the Snow Queen gone.

One night, Gerda had a terrible nightmare.

She was lost in the forest, shouting for Kay,
but he was so far away, he seemed to be in
another world.

There was a reindeer trying
to help her, but just as she was about
to touch it, she awoke with a start.

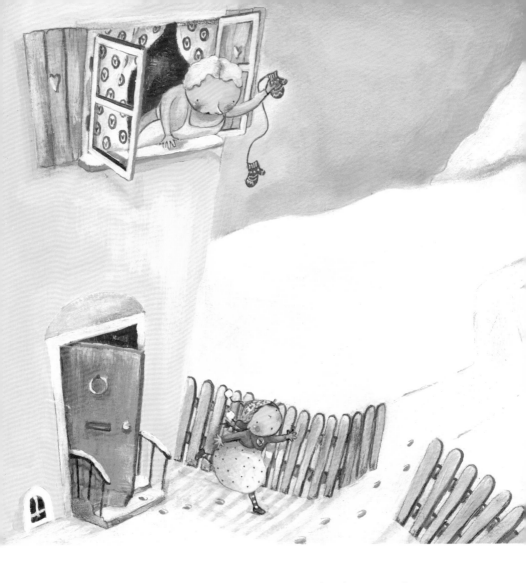

She hurried into her winter clothes and went outside to meet Kay. But he wasn't there.

Instead, there was only a set of wonky sledge tracks. Kay's sledge tracks. And instead of leading down to the lake, they were leading up into the frozen mountains.

Gerda rushed to Kay's door but when his
mother answered it she didn't know a boy
called Kay. No one knew a boy called Kay.

Gerda pictured Kay alone and afraid.
She knew what she had to do.

Gerda didn't think about how far she had
to go. She just followed the tracks,
thinking of her friend.

Snow began to fall, covering the tracks that
Kay's sledge had left. The harder she tried to
picture Kay's laughing face, the harder

the snow fell and the harder it became to
follow his tracks. Eventually, the snow
completely covered them.

She stood in the midst of a thicket of bracken
and nettles and could only guess which way
to go now.

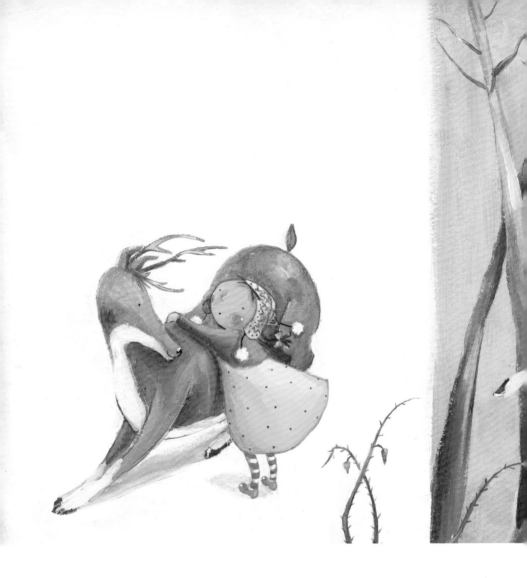

Just as she felt all hope drain from her,
something light moved in the darkness.

A reindeer! It was warm and seemed so
kind and gentle. Gerda was sure it was
the reindeer from her dream. It was trying
to help her.

She climbed onto its back and it leapt
forwards, carrying her easily over the uneven
frozen ground. They pushed further and further
into the mountains and just when Gerda
thought that they couldn't get any higher,
they turned a corner.

An enormous palace of ice came into view.

Gerda could only gasp. It was the Snow
Queen's palace. It was true. She took a deep
breath and thought of Kay.

How afraid he must be!

Then she set off alone across the frozen
wasteland, turning only to wave fondly at
the reindeer.

Sooner than she wished, Gerda was walking through the cold corridors of the Snow Queen's palace, silently padding over the frozen floor, desperately seeking Kay.

Strange noises echoed around the
empty halls.

Then, she saw something.

It was Kay. He was sitting on the cold floor,
staring into thin air. "Kay, it's me!" she cried.
But Kay just stared at her, confused.

"Kay!" Gerda cried, shaking him, but he
just looked at her blankly.

Gerda was helpless. She pulled at him, trying to drag him, but he was like a dead weight.

Finally, she fell to the floor, put her arms around her friend and sobbed.

But as she cried, her warm tears fell onto
Kay and something happened.

Kay's frozen heart began to melt, and the
Snow Queen's evil spell was lifted.
Finally he knew who she was.

Kay smiled and laughed at the sight
of his friend.

"You remembered me!"

Suddenly the Snow Queen appeared,
screaming and trying to grab Kay back
from Gerda.

"No!" she screeched wildly. "You cannot
take him! He's mine!"

She was furious, but when she tried to grab
Kay, he was so warm that her cold hands
burned as she touched him!

There was no time to waste! They sped
through the palace halls...

...and burst out into the fresh air.

The palace of ice had disappeared
and with it, the Snow Queen too.

She had been defeated! Never again
would she be able to steal children.

And no one ever forgot what
Gerda had done for her friend,
especially not Kay!

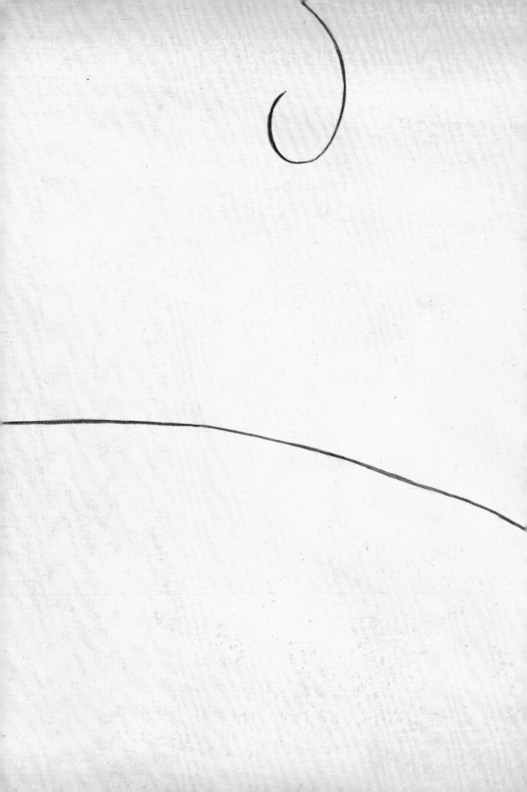

The Elves and the Shoemaker

Retold by Lucy M George and illustrated by Rachel Swirles

There once lived a talented shoemaker.

He lived with his wife in a little house,
above a little shop, in a little town,
above the rolling hills.

From far and wide, people came to buy
their beautiful shoes.

The Shoemaker would spend all day
drawing, cutting and stitching, filling the
shop with wonderful shoes.

His wife would spend all day helping,
searching and choosing, finding the perfect
pair of shoes for each customer.

Each person would leave with a pair of
shoes that fitted and suited them so perfectly,
it was as if the shoes had been made just
for them.

The years passed happily, and as they passed, the Shoemaker grew older.

But as he grew older, his fingers did too. He could no longer work as quickly as he had once been able to.

Soon, a day came when they sold their
last pair of shoes.

The Shoemaker could only afford
enough leather to make one last pair.

As the sun was setting, he carefully laid out the last of his material.

He cut out the pattern, paying attention to every last detail.

Then he left the work on his table and blew out his candle.

Together the Shoemaker and his wife climbed to bed with heavy limbs but faithful hearts.

At the crack of dawn, the Shoemaker got up and went straight to work.

But the leather had gone! In its place, there sat a pair of beautifully sewn, immaculately crafted, brand new shoes. They were flawless.

The Shoemaker was amazed and could only stare and admire the delicate work. The stitching was so fine, it was as if they had been crafted by magic.

That day the Shoemaker's wife sold the
shoes for twice the price she would normally
get. The couple were overjoyed.

The Shoemaker went straight out and bought twice as much leather as the day before.

He cut it out and they went to bed feeling encouraged and inspired.

The next morning, the Shoemaker went
down to his workshop with a spring in his step.

But when he got there, he was amazed
to see not one, but two extraordinary pairs
of brand new shoes!

Before lunch time, both pairs had been sold
for more than they had ever imagined possible.
The Shoemaker went out and bought enough
leather to fill the shop with shoes once more.
And for the rest of the day he carefully cut
out the leather.

That night, the Shoemaker and his wife decided to hide and watch. They would wait and discover who it was that was helping them so kindly.

They crept behind a curtain and silently waited. As the clock struck twelve, they heard the sound of distant voices singing, first softly, but getting closer.

Then in the dim light they saw…

…a group of tiny little elves!

They were dressed in ragged clothes,
their tiny feet completely bare.

With perfect grace and the lightest touch,
the elves seized the leather, the needles and
the thread and stitched and sewed and
worked their nimble little fingers so quickly
it was enchanting.

When all the work was done, the elves
clapped their hands and sang and danced
in a merry circle, skipping around the
shoes with glee.

Such cheerful creatures had never been seen.
Such joyful singing had never been heard.
Such handsome shoes had never been made!

There were now enough shoes to fill the
shop again.

The Shoemaker and his wife knew they had
to do something to show how grateful they
were. Then they had an idea.

They worked all day long, drawing,
cutting and sewing...

...until finally, when the sun had set, their
work was complete.

Late that night they went back to their
old hiding place and quietly waited.

As the clock struck twelve, they saw the elves, in their ragged old clothes, dance into the shop.

But when they reached the table, their singing suddenly stopped as it was replaced with excited chatter and squeals of joy.

On the table lay a tiny little outfit for each of them, and a pair of shoes each too!

When they were dressed, the elves began
to sing. They danced, admired each other,
and giggled and squealed!

How fine they all looked!

The couple watched with smiles of pride
as the elves, still giggling and dancing,
took off into the night.

The shop was flourishing again, filled with
beautiful shoes and excited customers...

...and the Shoemaker and his wife lived
happily once more!

But from then on, once in a while,
when the Shoemaker had a little spare
leather and a little spare time, he would
make a pair of tiny shoes and leave them
out for the elves…

...and sure enough, once in a while,
there would be a little surprise on the
Shoemaker's table in the morning!

Thumbelina, first published 2008
The Snow Queen, first published 2008
The Elves and the Shoemaker, first published 2009

This edition first published 2010 by Meadowside Children's Books,
185 Fleet Street, London, EC4A 2HS
www.meadowsidebooks.com

The right of Lucy M George and Rachel Swirles to be identified
as the author and illustrator of this work have been asserted by them
in accordance with the Copyright, Designs and Patents Act, 1988

A CIP catalogue record for this book is
available from the British Library

10 9 8 7 6 5 4 3 2 1

Printed in China